Published by Modern Publishing,
a Division of Unisystems, Inc.

Designed for Modern Publishing by Victoria
House Publishing Ltd., 4–5 Lower Borough Walls,
Bath, England

Printed in Belgium

THE ELEPHANT WHO FORGOT

Written by Stewart Cowley
Illustrated by Colin Petty

MODERN PUBLISHING
A Division of Unisystems, Inc.
New York, New York 10022

Tusker the Elephant's memory
Was really exceptionally fine.
He stood on the bank of a cool jungle stream
From eleven o'clock until nine.

And all the animals from the jungle
Who needed to know what he knew,
Could line up to ask his advice
In exchange for a peanut or two.

One morning a lizard came to wake him,
And cried, "Tusker, hurry! It's late!"
As Tusker started to climb out of bed,
He suddenly stopped and yelled, "Wait!"

Tusker tried to remember all the things that he knew,
And his heart immediately sank.
He couldn't remember a thing at all,
His mind had gone totally blank!

It was pride that stopped Tusker admitting
That he hadn't a fact in his head,
"So what if my memory's vanished," he thought,
"I'll just make up some answers instead."

"What shall I do," said the Hippo,
"To teach my young children to float?"
Tusker's advice was not very nice,
"Why bother? Just build them a boat!"

The Monkeys brought coconuts to him,
Saying, "How can we open all these?"
"Just drop them," said Tusker, "They'll fall to the ground,
And they'll break with the greatest of ease!"

The Gorillas' new carriage wasn't working,
One wheel just wouldn't turn round,
"Why bother to mend it, just pull off the rest,
And drag it over the ground."

And so, silly Tusker continued,
Getting everyone very confused.
Coconuts seemed to drop out of the sky
Making everyone battered and bruised.

When Tusker saw all the commotion,
He knew that he'd surely be blamed.
He ran away from all of his friends,
Feeling foolish and very ashamed.

"It's not his fault we're in trouble,"
Said the Rhino shaking his head.
"We've depended on Tusker to think for us all
And not solved our *own* problems instead."

They decided to bring Tusker home,
So they sawed and hammered and nailed,
To build a magnificent raft out of trees,
And down the river they sailed.

They got dizzy from spinning in the rapids,
It was like being stirred with a spoon.
Then at last they saw Tusker, looking very sad,
On the shore of a lonely lagoon.

"Come back, Tusker!" they cried,
"You can help us paddle back home.
It wasn't your fault we got everything wrong,
So you don't need to stay here alone."

"The Gorillas have mended their wheel
With string and considerable skill.
The Turtles are teaching the Hippos to swim
And the Monkeys invented a drill!"

So now all the beasts are quite proud,
Of the thinking they've learned to do.
And Tusker the Elephant's memory returned
To solve a problem or two.